READING CHAMPION

# THE BLITZ BABY

by Damian Harvey and Nicolas Hitori De

**W**

**FRANKLIN WATTS**

LONDON • SYDNEY

# THE BLITZ BABY

## CONTENTS

# CHAPTER 1

## AIR RAID

It was eight o'clock. The familiar wail of the air-raid siren filled the air.

"Not again. This is the second night in a row," said Mum. "Perhaps I should have taken Thomas and Jenny straight home after school."

"Don't worry," said Auntie Irene. "Donald's built a shelter in the back garden. He's working tonight, so there'll be plenty of room."

"I'd rather go home," said Jenny.

Mum shook her head. "No!" she replied. "We don't have time, and the public shelters will be crowded."

There wasn't much room in the Anderson shelter but it was better than being squeezed into a public one. It was also better than being outside like Uncle Donald, putting out fires.

It wasn't long before they heard the boom and thud of the anti-aircraft guns. Mum had been right, they wouldn't have had time to get anywhere else. Then came the heavy drone of aeroplane engines, followed by the whistle of falling bombs.

The newspapers were calling it the Blitz, the German word for lightning, and Thomas could understand why ... the flashes were blinding, the explosions were deafening and the ground shook around them.

Even with soil piled on top, the metal walls of the shelter didn't keep out much noise. It was terrifying. The German air force were aiming to bomb Plymouth's dockyards miles away, but nowhere was safe.

There was nothing to do now but wait. To pass the time, Thomas and Jenny played marbles. Thomas didn't remember falling asleep, but he must have done.

Mum said that they had even slept through the 'all clear'. When the children woke up, the thundering of bombs had gone and in its place they could hear the sound of police and fire brigade sirens.

It felt cold and damp in the shelter and Thomas couldn't wait to get outside. As he stretched, the door opened and daylight came streaming in. "Everyone alright in there?" It was Uncle Donald, his face smeared with blood. "It's just a scratch," he said, when he saw their worried faces. "But it was a bad raid last night."

# CHAPTER 2

# THE MORNING AFTER

The front windows of Auntie Irene's house had been smashed in the air raid, but that was nothing. Her neighbours hadn't been so lucky. Walking out on to the street was like entering an alien world.

Parts of the road were blocked with rubble. Some of the houses across the road were in ruins, their roofs caved in and walls collapsed. Others had been destroyed completely. Thomas could see a group of wardens searching for survivors. "I'd better help," said Uncle Donald. "There'll be no rest for me today."

"And we'd better head home," said Mum. "If we've still got one."

Walking down the road, Jenny and Thomas saw that not one single house had been left undamaged.

"I hope our house is all right," said Thomas.

"Me too," said Jenny.

As they headed towards the city centre, Jenny and Thomas found it hard to believe how different everything looked. Schools, shops, houses and factories had been destroyed by the bombs.

At the end of the road, they stopped to watch firemen spraying water on the church.

"What sort of people would do a thing like this?" asked Jenny. "I don't know," said Thomas. "The Germans must be monsters."

# CHAPTER 3

# THE BOMBER

Leaving the burning church behind, Mum led them towards the outskirts of the city. Some streets hadn't been damaged at all but others were in ruin.

"Look there," said Jenny, pointing.

The side of one house had completely gone and they could see inside. A bed was hanging out from a room on the top floor.

In the street, a man was rummaging through the rubble, seeing if there was anything he could salvage.

On the corner, they passed a caravan where a crowd of people had gathered to get water. Beyond that was a huge crater in the ground with the tangled remains of a bus poking out.

A warden was standing by the hole. "Good job no one was on board," he said, "but at least we got one of theirs."

"What do you mean?" asked Thomas.

"The guns took down a bomber," said the warden, pointing. "Crashed into the trees over there."

"That's near where we live," said Jenny.

"The plane's still there," said the warden. "If you're quick, you'll see it. The army will have removed all the dangerous stuff so it should be safe."

When they reached their street, they were relieved to see most of it had escaped the bombs. But one house was in ruins, and wardens were helping a family search through the remains, trying to salvage what they could.

"I'll see if I can help," said Mum.

"We're going to look at that plane," said Thomas excitedly.

"Just be careful," said Mum.

"Don't worry," said Thomas. "We will."

The houses near the end of the street were a mess, and the last one had been almost completely demolished. No one seemed to be searching there, so Thomas guessed the people who lived in them would have been evacuated before last night's raid.

As they reached the corner, the wreckage of the aeroplane came into sight. After being shot down, it had crash-landed in the trees behind their street. It must have only just missed their house. One of the aeroplane's wings was missing and the glass nose where the front gunner had sat was smashed.

"Look at the size of it!" cried Thomas.

"It's a Junkers 88," said Jenny.

"How do you know that?" asked Thomas.

Jenny grinned. "We saw a poster of them in school," she said.

"Come on," said Thomas. "Let's get a closer look."

He was about to go when Jenny stopped him.

"What was that?" she asked.

Thomas shrugged. "I didn't hear anything."

"It came from that house," said Jenny.

Then Thomas heard it too. "It sounds like a cat," he said. "Perhaps it's stuck."

15

# CHAPTER 4

## TRAPPED

The house was badly damaged and half of the roof had fallen in. Glass crunched beneath their feet as they headed towards the hole where the back door had once been. In the kitchen, they stopped to listen.

"There!" said Thomas. "It's definitely in here."

"I hope it's all right," said Jenny.

"Don't worry," Thomas assured her. "We'll find it."

In the next room, there was large hole in the floor and they could see down into the coal cellar. As they looked into the hole, the faint crying sound reached their ears again.

"It's coming from upstairs," said Thomas.

In the hallway, they stopped. The staircase to

the floor above had been partly destroyed

and only the top few steps remained.

Together, they dragged a sofa against the wall.

"We should be able to climb up this," said Thomas.

It was a bit wobbly but they managed to clamber

up the sofa and on to the floor above.

The faint sound of crying was coming from

the next room.

"It's in there," said Thomas, eagerly. "Come on!"

From the doorway, they saw that part

of the roof had collapsed from above.

At the far side they could see a wardrobe.


"I bet it's in there," said Thomas.

He made his way carefully across the room.

The floor creaked and groaned beneath his feet

but he finally made it to the other side.

Then he reached out and opened the wardrobe

door and let out a gasp.

"It's a baby!" he cried.

Jenny picked her way across to Thomas.

"What's a baby doing in there?"

"Someone must have put it there to keep it safe,"

said Thomas.

Jenny carefully picked the baby up. "I wonder where its mother is," she said.

"Let's take it to Mum," said Thomas. "She'll know what to do."

The two of them had barely taken a step when the floor began to creak and groan. The air was filled by the sound of splitting wood and there was a thunderous crash. Thomas cried out with pain.

When the dust cleared, they could see that
the floor had collapsed. They were left standing
on a small piece of floor by the wall. A plank
of wood had fallen on Thomas's leg.

"I can't move it," he said. "It's too heavy."

"What are we going to do?" asked Jenny.

"We're trapped!"

They tried shouting for help but it was no use.

"No one can hear us," said Thomas.

Then they heard noises coming from the stairs.

Jenny sighed with relief and smiled.

"Thank goodness," she said. "Someone did hear us."

But her smile soon disappeared.

Standing in the doorway was a man with a pistol

in his hand. And he was wearing a German uniform.

# CHAPTER 5

## FRIEND OR FOE?

Thomas had never been so frightened. His hands were shaking and his mouth was dry. He guessed that the man must have come from the crashed aeroplane.

"Please don't shoot," he begged. "We won't tell anyone we've seen you."

"Not a single word," added Jenny, her voice sounding wobbly and scared.

The man frowned and looked down at the pistol in his hand. Thomas felt sure that the German would pull the trigger at any moment.

Thomas was surprised to see a sad look cross the man's face. "No," he said, shaking his head. "I do not want to kill anyone. I am no murderer." Thomas didn't understand. "But you were on that plane," he said. "You dropped bombs on us."

The man sighed and nodded sadly. "My name is Franz Vogel," he said. "I am a pilot but I never wanted to fight. I was a pilot before this terrible war started. Hopefully I will still be a pilot when it is all over, too."

"I'm Jenny and this is Thomas," Jenny told him. "We don't know who the baby is."

Just then the small section of floor on which they were standing started to creak and groan.

"Quickly," said Franz. "We must get out now. The house could collapse at any moment."

"But we can't," cried Jenny. "Thomas is trapped."

Keeping close to the wall, Franz made his way around the edge of the room. One false step would have sent him tumbling through the hole in the floor. When he reached them, Franz struggled to lift the wood from Thomas's leg. As soon as it moved, Thomas wriggled free.

"Can you walk?" asked the pilot.

Thomas nodded. "It really hurts," he said. "But I think so."

"Good," said Franz. "Then follow me. Put your feet exactly where I put mine."

With the baby in his arms, Franz led the children past the hole in the floor. They made it out into the street just in time. No sooner had they left the house than it came crashing down behind them.

"That was close," said Thomas.

"Too close," agreed Franz.

The noise of the collapsing building brought air-raid wardens and soldiers running. Mum was just behind them. When they saw Franz, the soldiers raised their rifles.

Franz put his hands up in surrender.
"Wait!" shouted Thomas. "Don't shoot."
"Has he hurt you?" asked one of the soldiers.
"Of course not," said Thomas. "He rescued us. And this baby."

While the soldiers questioned Franz, Thomas and Jenny told Mum what had happened. As they did, a woman came forward to look after the baby.

"Are you her mother?" asked Mum.

"No, I'm her aunt. That was our family's house,"
said the woman, sadly. "I thought I'd lost them all."

"But what will happen to Franz?" asked Jenny.

"He's an enemy," explained Mum. "They'll take him to a prisoner of war camp."

"But he's not an enemy," said Thomas. "He's our friend."

When the soldiers started to lead Franz away, Thomas and Jenny waved. Franz stopped for a moment, then smiled. He just had time to wave back before climbing into an army truck.

"Will we see him again?" asked Jenny.

"Who knows?" said Mum. "Perhaps after the war is over."

As they walked home, a warden called to them.

"Probably be another raid tonight," he said.

"Make sure you go to your shelter."

"Not again," cried Thomas.

"At least we'll be together," said Mum.

"We're the lucky ones."

# Things to think about

1. What do you think it must have been like in the air-raid shelters during a raid?
2. How do you imagine Jenny, Thomas and their mother felt as they walked home?
3. What do you think Jenny and Thomas should have done when they heard the noise from inside the house?
4. What do they think that Franz will do when he finds them? Why?
5. Why does Thomas call Franz "his friend" at the end?

# Write it yourself

This story is set during the Second World War and involves many historical details from this time.

Now try to write your own story from a specific time in history. Plan your story before you begin to write it.

Start off with a story map:

• a beginning to introduce the characters and where and when your story is set (the setting);

• a problem which the main characters will need to fix in the story;

• an ending where the problems are resolved.

Get writing! Try to give your story a real sense of its historical setting. Research the time period to make sure your details are correct and really engage your reader in your story world.

# Notes for parents and carers

## Independent reading
The aim of independent reading is to read this book with ease. This series is designed to provide an opportunity for your child to read for pleasure and enjoyment. These notes are written for you to help your child make the most of this book.

## About the book
This story is set in Plymouth, UK, during a bombing raid of the Second World War. When Jenny and Thomas hear a noise from a bombed-out house, they decide to investigate. They discover a baby and are in turn discovered by a German pilot. His courage and friendship save the children's lives.

## Before reading
Ask your child why they have selected this book. Look at the title and blurb together. What do they think it will be about? Do they think they will like it?

## During reading
Encourage your child to read independently. If they get stuck on a longer word, remind them that they can find syllable chunks that can be sounded out from left to right. They can also read on in the sentence and think about what would make sense.

## After reading
Support comprehension by talking about the story. What happened? Then help your child think about the messages in the book that go beyond the story, using the questions on the page opposite. Give your child a chance to respond to the story, asking:
Did you enjoy the story and why? Who was your favourite character? What was your favourite part? What did you expect to happen at the end?

Franklin Watts
First published in Great Britain in 2019
by The Watts Publishing Group

Series Editors: Jackie Hamley and Melanie Palmer
Series Advisors: Dr Sue Bodman and Glen Franklin
Series Designer: Peter Scoulding

A CIP catalogue record for this book is
available from the British Library.

ISBN 978 1 4451 6507 3 (hbk)
ISBN 978 1 4451 6508 0 (pbk)
ISBN 978 1 4451 6842 5 (library ebook)

Printed in China

Franklin Watts
An imprint of
Hachette Children's Group
Part of The Watts Publishing Group
Carmelite House
50 Victoria Embankment
London EC4Y 0DZ

An Hachette UK Company
www.hachette.co.uk

www.franklinwatts.co.uk

FSC
www.fsc.org
MIX
Paper from
responsible sources
FSC® C104740